Gigi & Jacques' Starry Night in Paris

written & illustrated by
Maureen Edgecomb

PUBLISHED EXCLUSIVELY

for

LAS VEGAS

Published in the United States 2003
by Ravenwood Studios
P.O. Box 197
Diamond Springs, California 95619

Exclusively for
Park Place Entertainment Corporation

Gigi Paris and Jacques are trademarks of Park Place Entertainment Corporation

Book Design by Ruth Marcus, Sequim, WA

Printed in Hong Kong

First Edition

ISBN #0-9718604-3-2

It was springtime in Paris, and the whole world was in love . . .

...but especially along the Champs Elysées...

…and in Montmartre.

Gigi and Jacques
and Claudette and
Philippe spent much
of their time together…

going to romantic places…
walking paw-in-paw,
hand-in-hand.

Jacques always impressed Gigi with his
savoir-faire.
"I can get us into high places, mon cheri,"
he claimed.

Philippe gave Claudette
beautiful flowers,

*pour vous,
mon petite fleur*

so Jacques gave some to Gigi, too.

Gigi adored Jacques' finesse!

Philippe said if you toss a coin in the Place de la Concorde fountain, your wish would come true.

So, Jacques thought a bone would be even luckier,
but he forgot to let go.

Philippe loved to paint, especially beautiful subjects like Claudette.
Jacques wanted Philippe to paint a portrait of Gigi, too.

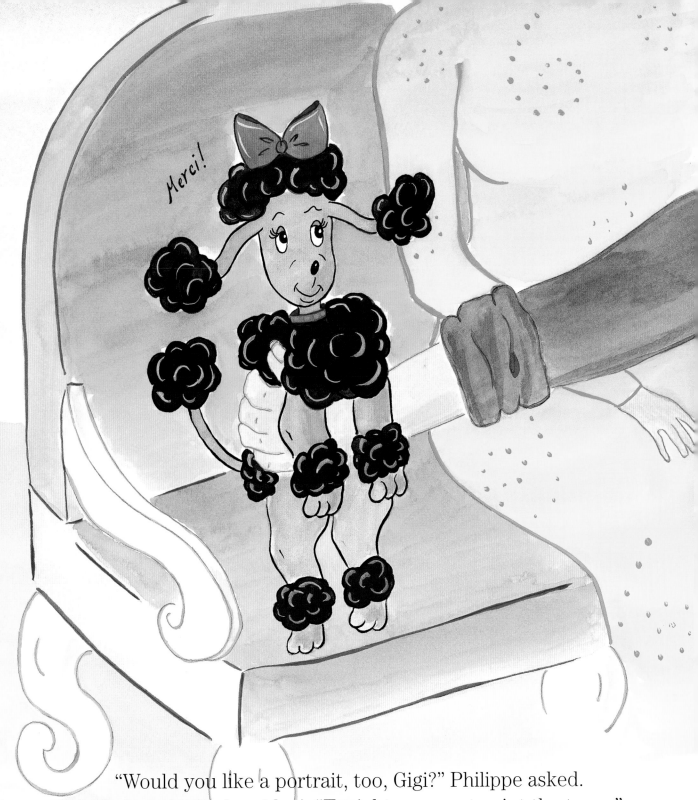

"Would you like a portrait, too, Gigi?" Philippe asked.
Just then, he had an idea! "Tonight, we must paint the town,"
Philippe exclaimed, "we have all of Paris, and the night is young!"

So, they all jumped into Philippe's car and set out for a night in Paris.

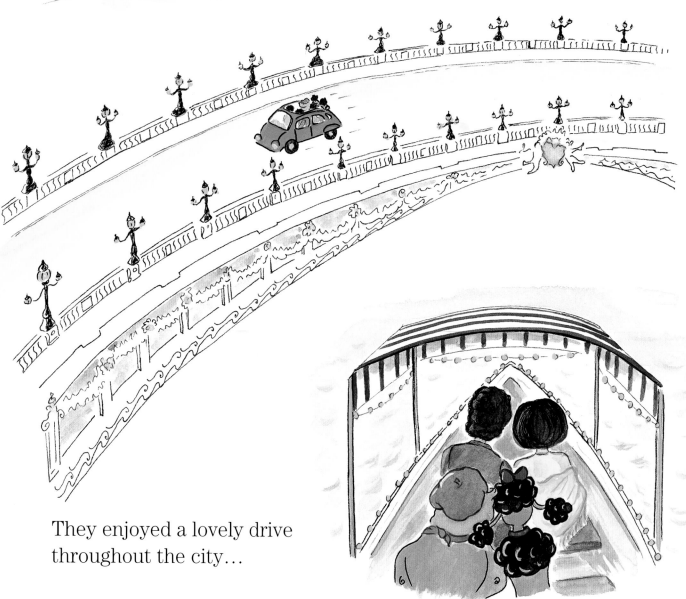

They enjoyed a lovely drive throughout the city…

and a romantic boat ride down the Seine.

Then to a fun park and a ride on the Ferris wheel!
Gigi and Jacques rode all by themselves and saw
all of Paris from the top!

But Claudette and Philippe were so much in love
they only saw each other, and they forgot about Gigi and Jacques.
They wandered off, hand-in-hand into the crowd.

Poor Jacques and Gigi couldn't follow. They were stuck at the top!
"You really know how to get us into high places, Jacques," Gigi barked.

"We lost them, Jacques! It is not possible, c'est impossible! We must be more careful! Dogs of good breeding stay with their masters," Gigi scolded.

Jacques answered, "Maybe when all the people leave, we'll find them. For now, let's have fun, Gigi. We have all of Paris, and the night is young!"

"Bonsoir, Strudel.
Have you seen Claudette and Philippe?"
"No, Jacques and Gigi," Strudel answered.
"Have you seen them, Oscar?"
"No, Strudel," Oscar purred, "but I know a pur-r-r-r-fect place to begin our search!"
So, together, they set off to look for Claudette and Philippe.

They looked in a famous nightclub…

...a familiar café...

and found more of their friends.

"Bonsoir, Cookie and Dandy Man.
Have you seen Claudette and Philippe?"
Gigi asked.

"No mon amies, but let's
ask Tallulah."

"Tallulah, have you seen Jacques' and Gigi's master and mistress?"
"No, Dandy. Je regretter, I'm sorry. But, together we will look."

"Pardonnez-moi. Have you seen this poodle?" Claudette asked.
"Oui, mademoiselle. She was with a handsome bulldog.
Oui, and others, over there."

Just then, Jacques and Gigi found themselves in the middle of
an outdoor dance floor. "Welcome to the Stardust Club,
Mesdames et Monsieurs. Let the evening begin!"

Balloons fell from above and popped, spilling shiny confetti
all over the floor!

The lights went out and all the confetti lit up the floor
like stars in the night sky!

As they left the dance floor, they continued their search, but Jacques was becoming sad.

"I'm sorry I get us lost so much, Gigi," he sighed.

"Jacques, why couldn't you see we were getting lost?"

"I could only see you, Gigi." Jacques whispered.

"Oh, Jacques," Gigi replied, "You are so sweet!"

Just then, Philippe saw Jacques' trail!
"Look! Jacques left us a trail!"
Claudette and Philippe ran fast until they saw their beloved
Jacques and Gigi just ahead.

Gigi barked for joy, and Jacques danced in circles!
Claudette and Philippe laughed with delight.

Philippe exclaimed, "Your trail of confetti did it, Jacques.
You are the smartest dog in all of Paris! If it wasn't for you…"

Jacques blushed. Gigi was so very proud of him.

Jacques looked into Gigi's eyes and sighed, "I always get us lost."
"Oh, no—au contraire, Jacques. You are my hero, mon champion.
You always get us found!"

And they all went back home to Philippe's studio for the
happiest ending to the best starry night in all of Paris!